A Space for Me

Cathryn Falwell

Lee & Low Books Inc. • New York

Edited by Louise E. May
Designed by David and Susan Neuhaus/NeuStudio
Production by The Kids at Our House
The text is set in 21-point Arquitecta Bold
The illustrations are rendered in cut paper collage

Manufactured in China by Toppan
10 9 8 7 6 5 4 3 2 1
First Edition

Library of Congress Cataloging-in-Publication Data
Names: Falwell, Cathryn, author, illustrator.
Title: A space for me / by Cathryn Falwell.
Description: First edition. | New York : Lee & Low Books Inc, [2020] |
Summary: "Alex wants some space for himself away from his younger brother
who takes his things and makes noise, but eventually Alex finds a way to make
space for his brother too"— Provided by publisher.
Identifiers: LCCN 2019024950 | ISBN 9781620149638 (hardcover)
Subjects: CYAC: Brothers—Fiction. | Personal space—Fiction.
Classification: LCC PZ7.F198 Sp 2020 | DDC [E]—dc23
LC record available at https://lccn.loc.gov/2019024950

It's not fair.
My big sister, Emma,
has her own room,
but I have to share a room
with my little brother.
Lucas is a pain.
He takes my stuff
and makes noise
and plays on my side
of the room, in my space.
It's not fair!

I put tape on the floor
and tell Lucas,
"That side is your space,
and this side is mine.
My space."

But Lucas forgets—
all the time.

Today Lucas knocked over
the tower I was building,
broke my favorite dragon,
spilled the crayon basket,
and tossed all the pieces
of a puzzle up in the air.

I've had enough!
I go outside to look
for a space all my own.

I see a space
by my favorite tree.
I find fallen branches
and an old broom
and a broken chair.
I pull over my wagon.

Emma sees me
and comes outside.
"Can I help, Alex?" she asks.
"I'm making a space
where I can be by myself," I say.
"You can help me find a roof."

"Let's go inside and look
in the give-away box," says Emma.
I pull out an old towel.
"This will be perfect," I say.

I like having a space
just for me.
I listen to the birds
making chirpy sounds.
I think and dream
of magical things.

One day I see Lucas watching me
from our bedroom window.
He looks sad.
Why is he sad?
He has the whole room to himself.

I look away, but Lucas still watches me.
A squirrel climbs my tree.
A grasshopper twitches its legs.

I leave my quiet space
and go to our room.
"Lucas, why are you sad?
You have our whole room
for yourself," I say.

"But I want to be with you," says Lucas.

We are both quiet for a little while.
Then I have an idea.
"Come on," I say.

We go outside and spend
the rest of the afternoon
making a space for Lucas.

Some days I spend time
in my space all by myself.

Some days Lucas plays
in his space all by himself.

And some days we play together.

Lucas and I still share a room.

And sometimes
it's a space
for both of us.

MAR   2020